DJ
DREAMBOAT

E J BRADDOCK

Copyright © 2025 Emma J Braddock

All rights reserved.

The events and characters in this book are complete works of fiction. Any similarity to real persons either living or dead are coincidental and are not intended by the author.

No part of this book may be reproduced, replicated, distributed or transmitted in any form by any mechanical or electrical means, including information storage and retrieval systems, without the express permission in writing from the publisher, except by a reviewer who may quote brief passages in a review.

Contents

Dedication	1
Foreword	2
Acknowledgements	3
1. CHAPTER 1	4
2. CHAPTER 2	15
3. CHAPTER 3	21
4. CHAPTER 4	29
5. CHAPTER 5	35
6. CHAPTER 6	39
7. CHAPTER 7	46
8. CHAPTER 8	51
9. CHAPTER 9	55
10. CHAPTER 10	64
Afterword	68

Dave

Thank you for being you, you are an amazing friend

Here's my addition for your Indie bookshelf

E.J. Braddock

For all the Gen X's that grew up with the best generation of music
80's rock/punk

FOREWORD

Welcome to my debut novella. Initially this was a side project that I never intended to publish, but after a friend of mine read it she encouraged me to release it into the wild.

Dreams are the mind's way of processing our day to day life and our memories, through our sub consciousness while we sleep.

Many times, I wake from a dream and think, 'Oh, I must write that down, it will make a great short story.' More often than not, by the time I get access to my laptop, or pen and paper, the dream has gone. This dream, however, managed to stick.

So please enjoy the ramblings of my unconscious mind in.
DJ DREAMBOAT

ACKNOWLEDGEMENTS

I would like to thank the amazing Alexia Muelle- Rushbrook for her help while I wrote, edited and formatted this novella. Her insights and advice has been invaluable.

I would also like to thank the wonderful Megan G Mossgrove. Her live writing sprints on TikTok have been instrumental in keeping me focused and keeping my mind from wandering off task.

I of course have to thank the wonderful Tom Mutinyz, the TikTok DJ who inspired the musical theme for the book.

And last but not least my wonderful friend David W Adams who has been my sounding board, and a walking encyclopaedia of knowledge pertaining to all things indie publishing. Thank you for always being at the end of a message whenever I needed to ramble or query something.

If you would like to follow Alexia, Megan, David or myself on social media feel free to look us up. Our TikTok handles are:

@alexia_muelle_rushbrook
@mossgrovewrites
@davidwadams.author
@Mutinyz
And myself @Emma B author

Chapter 1

It's Saturday night and I've been dragged out by my best friend, Laney, to an 80's party at the house of some bigwig internet D.J. I really don't want to go, but I promised her I would show my face and stay for a couple of songs at least.

So here I am, doing my best friend a solid, when what I really want to be doing is ordering Chinese and vegetating on the sofa with Netflix. She said the dress code was 80's optional so I opted out kind of. Instead I put on my smartest skinny jeans, black ankle biker boots and my Gun's N Roses t-shirt. I figured cos they were an 80's band I'd fit in, right?

When I arrived at the party and it was heaving. I nearly turned right back around and left, but Laney saw me as she was coming out for a quick smoke. Damn her and her filthy habit. I plastered the biggest smile on my face I could muster and walked towards the door. Laney put out her smoke, walked me inside and led me through to the main room.

Classic 80's music was blaring out of the speakers. Don't get me wrong I love the music from the 80's. I just don't like parties. I especially hate being coerced into going to them. The room was massive. It looked like they'd knocked all the bottom floor rooms together and just kept the support beam posts.

At the back of the room stood what I assume used to be a bar that had been turned into a D.J booth. The D.J was wearing

DJ DREAMBOAT

one of those loud Hawaiian shirts that were made popular in the late 50's, back when tourism took off in the state of Hawaii. There were L.E.D globe lights dotted across the top of the large squared U-shaped bar. large colour changing tube lights framed the wall behind the D.J. illuminating him and his equipment in a very 80's night club setting.

Other light tubes were positioned vertically along the side walls. Each one changing colours from red to blue into green and purple in a constant loop. The dance floor itself was heaving with gyrating bodies. The men clearly flaunting themselves like peacocks trying to mate. It was laughable, they clearly had no clue as to what women think is attractive in a man. Sad really.

The song changed to a slower tempo and as I looked toward the D.J he waved me over. I was confused but went over anyway.

"Hey there princess. You're new to my parties, aren't you?"

"Erm, yeah I am."

"Cool, what's your favourite 80s song? I'll play it just for you to honour your first time here."

"Well I don't have a particular favourite, but I have a favourite

type of music, so if there's any 80's rock in your playlist, that would be cool. Surprise me!"

"Will do princess, I know just the thing."

To say I was nervous was an understatement, what had I gotten myself into and how soon could I get myself out of it?

"Ok folks we're going to rock it back up for you now with a special request from our newcomer. So, rev up your engines and get down and dirty to my very own mash up. Enjoy."

The instrumental for *Sweet Child of Mine* starts blasting out of the speakers and I turn to him and scream thank you. He chuckles and carries on with his thing. I'm back to getting my groove on when in blends the vocals for *Madonna's* hit *Papa Don't Preach* with *Sweet Child*.

I was totally confused yet loving it. I happily swayed along to two of the most iconic 80's songs. There was a danger I would actually enjoy being here. As the music faded into the next song I looked toward him and gave him a thumbs up. He gave me a cheeky wink and waved me over.

"So, princess, did you like the surprise?"

"It was intense. I loved it. I wouldn't have thought those would have worked together, but it was amazing. What made you think of mashing them together? And why those in particular?"

"I got the idea for *Sweet Child* from your t-shirt and you don't seem like the type of woman who lets others tell her what to do. The rest is a trade secret going way back."

"Oh wow, I thought it might have been a new thing that maybe came out of the flu pandemic, we had a few years back."

"Don't get me started on those wanna be laptop bedroom DJ's."

"Touchy subject, got it, Oh, and by the way, *Tom Selleck* called he wants his shirt back."

"Cheeky lil minx."

I had no idea where Laney had disappeared to. She was probably chatting up someone. She was never one to be short of admirers or attention, always the life and soul of any party she went to. Our conversation was cut short by a fight that was breaking out between a couple of idiots who had clearly drunk way too much.

"Hey princess watch the decks for me, while I go sort out these reprobates."

"I don't know what to do!"

"When this song's done press the flashing button. I won't belong."

DJ DREAMBOAT

I didn't have time to argue with him, he was off. I stepped behind the bar and looked in panic for a flashing button. I managed to find it just as the song ended, pressed it, and another song began in place of the last. Phew that was close. I looked up, gave the D.J the thumbs up as he was escorting the miscreants out by the scruffs of their necks. The song was nearly over when he came back in, looking dishevelled. His ash blonde hair was no longer neat and there was a tear in his shirt.

"Thanks, princess, I can take over now."

"What about your shirt?"

Looking down, he swore under his breath, bent down, and picked up a box from under the bar. To my surprise it was filled with more Hawaiian shirts. I thought he was going to pick one out and ask me to look after things again, while he went to change; but no, he just took his shirt off right there in front of me. I didn't know where to look, man he was hot.

"Like what you see, princess?"

"Yes, erm I mean, well, what I mean is you, are,"

Damn it woman, get your act together. You're practically drooling.

"You're even cuter when you get embarrassed."

Great, he'd noticed, slick move Ange. He gave me one of his winks, bent down and kissed me on my cheek, I was gone. Puddling in my panties, lusting after a total stranger with musical talent to die for, and a strange habit of calling me princess. I spent the rest of the evening standing next to his booth talking to him, admiring his chest, and trying my best to keep it together. At 11:00 p.m. we said our goodbyes.

He'd insisted on swapping phone numbers, giving the excuse that it was so he could contact me with details of further events he had planned. I didn't give it much thought though as I was preoccupied with finding Laney. I eventually found her draped over some very drunk ne'er do well. The walk home sobered me up, but Laney was still three sheets to the wind, so I insisted she stay the night at my place.

She didn't need much convincing and ended up passing out on the sofa before I'd even taken my boots off. We slept in till noon the next day and Laney went home around 1:00 p.m. to get changed ready for Sunday dinner at her parent's house. After a quick trip to the supermarket before it closed I spent the rest of the day cleaning.

The next week passed in a blur of work and daydreaming about the D.J.

I hadn't told anyone about what happened that night, not that they would've believed me anyway; why would they? I'm a plain jane, he's a handsome D.J, who could have his pick of beautiful women. He wouldn't think once about me let alone twice.

Laney would have believed me, she would also have teased me endlessly about him, and insist on dragging me to his next event. Saturday morning came around again and I woke to a voicemail, I half listened to it expecting it to be from my brother Michael; so, you can imagine how shocked I was to hear D.J dreamboat's voice.

"Hi, princess, It's J.T the D.J from the party last weekend. I don't know if you remember me, but I'm having another get together tonight, at the same place. It starts at 7:30 p.m. I'd love it if you could come. Hope to see you there, bye."

I couldn't believe it, I was floating on cloud nine all day. If my mother had seen me, she would've had me tested for drugs. Around 5:00 p.m. I ran myself a hot bubble bath and had a long soak in the tub, thinking about my D.J. At 6:30 p.m. I put on my sexiest knee length red dress. The material hugged my figure perfectly and the plunging neckline showed off my girls to their fullest.

DJ DREAMBOAT

It had a slit that ran from the hem line all the way up to the top of my outer left thigh. I paired it with a pair of matching blood red kitten heels and a drop pendant necklace that rested in the dip of my cleavage.

I pinned my hair up in a messy bun, leaving ringlets framing the edge of my face, and the odd tendril running down the back of my neck. I was nervous but also excited. Grabbing my silver chained handbag and my keys, I walked out the door and set off to catch me my D.J prince. When I got to the house it was dark and quiet. I was beginning to think that it was all a trick. I decided however to give him the benefit of the doubt and sent him a text.

Hi, it's Angela, your princess! I'm outside but there doesn't appear to be anyone else here, am I too early?

Slipping my phone back into my bag, I was going to stick around for a few minutes then go home. The second I fastened the clasp on my bag my phone beeped.

Well hello princess! I'm here, just putting the finishing touches to everything. Party doesn't start for another half an hour. Come on through. The doors unlocked.

I headed straight to the back room. I could see he was setting up his equipment and took a moment to enjoy the view. He had his back to me bent over a crate, and boy was his backside as good looking as his front. His jeans fitted in all those perfect places, and yes, he was wearing yet another of those god-awful shirts, but if I had my way he wouldn't be wearing it for long.

"Are there any of those shirts left in Hawaii or have you bought them all?"

Slick Ange, real slick. He turned to face me, took one look at me, and wolf whistled, he actually bloody whistled at me.

"Wow, just wow! You're, breath-taking."

"Oh, this old thing? I've not worn this in years, I dug it out especially for you. I thought I could be your lady in red tonight."

He was drooling and staring at my breasts. I'd definitely chosen the right dress. I was hoping he would like it, though I wasn't prepared for his reaction.

"Eyes are up here cowboy,"

"I'm sorry, I don't normally behave like this, I, erm, I, well what I mean is."

But he didn't have time to finish what he was trying to say, as a stream of people made their way into the room and we got separated. When I caught glimpses of him during the night, he was always looking at me with lust in his eyes.

I don't know if it was the alcohol, the dress, or the rush of dopamine I get from his reaction to my dress, but whatever it was, I was more confident in that moment than I had ever been in my life. I danced, drank, and sang to the music, all the while undressing him with my eyes every time our eyes met.

A few guys came on to me, asking me to dance with them, so I did. Call me a bad girl, but I wanted to make him jealous, and it worked. After I went to the ladies to touch up my makeup, he was waiting for me outside the door, and me being the clutz I am I stumbled right into him. Grasping me around my waist, he steadied me with his right hand and cupped my neck with his left.

"Steady there, princess. You falling for me already? I haven't been able to take my eyes off of you all night I-"

"You what?"

"This."

Pulling me into him, he claimed my mouth with his; parting my lips with his tongue. The kiss became urgent, his left hand slipped down from my neck and onto my chest, stroking it across my breast, lifting it slightly, teasing me. The tingle danced from his fingertips through me to my core. I was putty in his hands, his to command. Slowing the kiss, he pulled away from me, searching my eyes for answers, to unasked questions.

My core was erupting. I could feel my black lace panties becoming wetter by the second. The control this man had over my loins was unbelievable. I ran my fingers through his hair, pulling him close to me once more, trailing kisses from his earlobe down to his shirt neckline, he growled in response with carnal desire.

"I've wanted to do that to you all week, princess."

"You have me now."

"God help me, this party can't end quick enough. Afterwards you're mine."

He reluctantly let me go. Turning around I went back into the bathroom to refresh my lipstick and slip my now ruined underwear into my handbag. When I re-entered the throng of gyrating bodies, I could tell he was following me with his gaze, staring at my ass.

"Ok folks, due to technical difficulties, the party is finishing early tonight, so you've got a couple of songs left before we call it a night. Sorry folks."

There was a collective sigh of disappointment from amongst the crowd. I smiled to myself, a few songs were all that stood between me and heaven. I danced those last songs, like there wasn't a care in the world. Guys came up to me and tried it on. I danced with them, making them think they had a chance with me, but in reality, I belonged to only one.

As the last song ended he said his goodbyes to everyone and wished them a safe journey home. When the last person had left, he locked the door, turned, and walked towards me; unbuttoning his shirt with each step he took, finally flinging it across the room.

When he reached me, I placed my hands on his chiselled chest, as he closed the gap between us. I left soft kisses on his upper chest, while snaking my hands up into his hair. Then there it was, the primal groan; accompanied with his soldier standing to attention, straining for release through his jeans.

"Woman you're driving me wild, I need you so bad."

"Then you'd better take me."

He swept me off my feet, I cupped my hands around his neck, as he carried me through the building and up the stairs. I whispered in his ear all the dirty thoughts I'd had running through my head all week. He growled, he actually growled.

"If you carry on talking to me like that princess we won't make it to the bedroom."

"Who needs a bedroom? Take me now."

He didn't need telling twice, placing me gently on the landing floor he stood up, kicked off his shoes, and unfastened his jeans. I lay there watching him strip as I licked my lips thinking of all the wicked things I wanted to do to him, and what I wanted him to do to me. Climbing on top of me he slid his long slender finger into my dripping wet pussy, fondling my clit with his thumb. I arched my back, moaning as he worked his magic with his fingers, while tickling, rubbing, and teasing my clit with his thumb.

"Oh yes princess, you like that don't you!"

"Yes, Yes, don't stop, do, o,o,n't sto.o.o.p, oh god, oh god, yes, yes!"

"Oh, I don't intend to. You're mine, now and always."

Slipping out his fingers he placed them into his mouth, licking them, devouring their scent, a devilishly wicked grin flashed across his gorgeous face.

"Open wide princess."

I didn't need telling twice. Placing his hand either side of me; he plunged himself deep inside me. He was mine and I was his. Slowly he built up the friction sliding in and out; driving me to the point of eruption. Slowly reaching down with his hand massaging me with his finger, I thought I was going to explode. He released his hand and returned to a faster thrust, calling my name over and over as we climaxed together. He collapsed next to me in exhaustion, moments later he leant on his elbow and caressed my breasts with his free hand.

"You know if we made it to the bedroom I could show you how wicked we could really be."

"What are you waiting for?"

Standing up, he helped me to my feet; held my hand and guided me along the hall. Once we were in the room we didn't leave until late afternoon the next day. We spent the time locked away in our love nest fucking, sleeping, and fucking some more. By late teatime we were ravenous for food instead of each other.

Hurting in places I didn't know I had, I could barely stand, let alone walk. Making my way gingerly to the bathroom, I ran a bath while he went to the kitchen to make us something to eat. The long soak in the tub was just what I needed to relax my aching new-found muscles.

As I got out of the bath my phone started ringing. I didn't recognise the number but answered it anyway, because my brother had a habit of breaking his phone and calling from temporary numbers until he had his fixed.

"Hello, Miss Marsh?"

"Yes, this is Miss Marsh, with whom am I speaking please?"

"This is Dr Green from the District General Hospital. I got your number from a Mr M Marsh. Could you tell me what relation you are to him please?"

"He's my brother. Wait did you say doctor? And hospital? Is he?"

"Yes, my name is Dr Green from the District General Hospital. No, your brother is not dead. He has however been in a road traffic accident."

"You are in his mobile as his emergency contact and next of kin. Could you come to the hospital as soon as possible please?"

"Yes of course, I can be there in an hour."

"Thank you, Miss Marsh, I will see you soon. Go straight to I.C.U and tell the nurse at the desk who you are and who"

"You're there to see. I will let her know she's to expect you." I hung up and dropped my phone, just as J.T came walking back in the room carrying a breakfast tray laden with pancakes, Nutella, and bacon. He took one look at me, placed the tray on the dresser and rushed to my side.

Chapter 2

"What's wrong princess? You look white as a sheet."

"That was a doctor at the hospital. It's my brother. There's been an accident. I, I need to be there as soon as I can, the doctor is expecting me. I'll call you tomorrow."

"Nonsense. You can't go on your own, you're a mess. I'll drive you, which hospital is it?"

"Erm I think he said District. You don't have to though really. I can walk home get changed and take a taxi there."

"Don't be silly. I insist; besides, you can't go back to yours wearing that dress and no underwear. I'll dig you out a pair of joggers and a t-shirt. Give me a few mins to grab a quick shower and get dressed then we can set off."

"Thank you, James. You hardly know me, let me know if I can ever repay the favour."

"I think we've gotten to know each other pretty well this weekend, but I know what you mean."

He told me to look through the bottom drawer in the dresser for something to wear while he had his shower. I found a pair of light grey joggers and an oversized *AC/DC* t-shirt; got dressed and went downstairs into the event room to wait for him. It wasn't long before he came in carrying my dress, handbag, and phone.

"That's a good look on you, princess."

"Very funny, James. I'm sure I look sexy as hell."

"I'm serious princess, you'd look sexy in a bin bag, come on my van's parked out front. I can take you home to change or I can take you straight to the hospital. It's completely up to you."

"I'd like to go straight to the hospital, if you don't mind."

"Your chariot awaits princess."

We drove to the hospital in silence. As soon as we got there I ran through the main entrance, found the floor that I.C.U was on, located the nearest lift and got off at the third floor. My mind was racing with all kinds of terror, scared of what I would find and what state Michael would be in.

"Can I help you miss?"

"Yes, I'm Angela Marsh. A Dr Green is expecting me."

"Ah yes, you must be Mr Marsh's sister. The doctor did mention you would be on your way; unfortunately, he's in surgery at the moment. Can I get you anything to drink? Tea? Coffee?"

"Do you have a water machine? I daren't have any caffeine. I'm a bundle of nerves as it is."

Five minutes later James came and sat next to me. I was staring off into nowhere, he made me jump when I felt his body brush against mine as he sat next to me.

"What are you doing here? I thought you were going to go straight back after dropping me off."

"I couldn't leave my princess in her hour of need. What kind of knight would I be if I did that?"

"Thank you, Sir James."

"Don't mention it. Have they said anything?"

"No, the doc is still in surgery. I'm waiting for him to come see me."

We talked for what seemed ages; getting to know each other to pass the time until the doctor came to find me. At some point I fell asleep on his shoulder.

"Hey, *Sleeping Beauty*, wake up; the docs here."

"What? Oh, hello, Doctor. How is he?"

"Hello Miss Marsh, thank you for coming so quickly; I'm sorry I kept you waiting. What I have to discuss with you can only be discussed with family, so I'm afraid unless this young man is another relation to Mr Marsh or he is your life partner, he will have to leave while I speak to you."

"Oh, right, erm James isn't, well I don't really know what he is."

"Then I'm afraid he will have to go take a walk, he is free to come back and stay with you after we have done talking."

"Thank you, Doctor."

"It's ok princess, I need to stretch my legs anyway. I left my mobile in the van. I'll go get it and wait for you to text me."

He stood up and lent down placing a gentle loving kiss on my forehead, before walking off down the corridor.

"So, then, Dr Green; what could you not tell me in front of James? And has anyone called our mother?"

"Well, you see. Michael was in a serious R.T.C, involving a log carrier and another car. It would appear the log carrier braked suddenly and lost a few of its load. Your brother was in the vehicle directly behind the truck and well, one of the logs landed on his bonnet. The car behind him crashed into the back of him and compacted his car, crushing his legs."

"Oh my God! I think I'm going to be sick."

"Nurse, fetch a sick bowl immediately please."

"Yes, Doctor."

"As you know he was still in the operating room when you arrived. There was a complication during the surgery and I'm afraid he's lost a lot of blood."

"What kind of complication?"

"Your brother's blood wouldn't clot and the damage sustained to his legs was too severe. I'm afraid we had to amputate both legs just above the knee. The next 24 hours are critical, if he survives the night then there's a good chance he will pull through, but he will be in a wheelchair for the rest of his life."

"Holy crap, wait you didn't answer my question about our mother."

"Your brother was drifting in and out of consciousness when he arrived, what little we could get out of him was your name and absolutely under no circumstances were we to contact his mother. You are named on his *in case of emergency card* that we found in his wallet."

I think I would have fainted if I hadn't already been sat down.

The nurse came back with a cardboard sick bowl, and the doctor made his apologies once more.

"I need to see him, NOW!"

"I'm afraid that's not possible at the moment, he is still sleeping off the anaesthetic. As soon as he's awake and lucid we will take you to him, but until then I'm afraid you will have to be patient."

The nurse went back to her desk and I took out my phone and texted James.

It's me, the doc's gone I'm going to go up to the canteen till Michael wakes up.

I waited for a reply but didn't get one. I figured the phone thing was an excuse to get the hell out of there, I'd probably never see him again. I managed to find my way up to the canteen; when I got there the food selection looked like it had been devoured by a swarm of locusts. The staff were clearing away what little there was left.

"Excuse me! Before you clear that away could I have some please?"

"Sure, thing honey, what would you like? There isn't much left though what you see is what we got."

"I'll have the cottage pie please; with chips and gravy, and is that a jam roley poley I spy over there?"

"It is honey, would you like some?"

"Oooo yes please. Could you warm it up for me?"

"Sure can. I'll keep it under the hot plate until you're ready for it, then I'll give it a zap in the microwave for ya."

"Brilliant, thank you."

"No problem, just wait for me at the till and I'll be right there."

I did as she asked and looked around the deserted canteen.

Cleaners were mulling around, wiping down the tables and chairs with those god awful smelling antibacterial sprays. Their cloths looked like they were ready for the incinerator.

"Right then honey, there you go. that'll be £7.90 please."

I gave her a tenner and pocketed what little bit of change there was; picking up my tray, I found the cleanest table I could, but it turned out to be a wonky little thing, so I used the paper napkins from on the table to level it off and proceeded to eat, what passed as close to food, as this place got.

The cleaner gave me the side eye a few times. I was unsure as to the reason why but decided it wasn't worth wasting time thinking about it. Although the food looked less than appetising it was actually delicious. I particularly liked the mash, I expected it to be lumpy but it was well mashed and tasted fluffy and creamy, perfect just the way I liked it.

Ten minutes later I was tucking into the jam roley poley and custard, the custard was a little watery but the sponge pudding was delicious. When I'd emptied the bowl of its delightful contents I cleared the table and bid the staff a good evening. I still hadn't received any communication from James; I assumed he had gone back to his place, writing the whole weekend off as a huge mistake. I couldn't blame him really, if it was the other way round I'd be running for the hills.

Still, it was best to find out now before I became too invested with my feelings. As I was muddling it all over my mobile rang.

Checking the caller I.D I didn't recognise the number, but as it was a landline I figured it was the nurse ringing with news about Michael.

"Is he awake?"

"Hi princess, it's me, sorry I couldn't text back; my mobile up and died on me. I didn't have my charger wire in the van, so I came home to charge it. The bloody thing's on its last legs. Thankfully when you gave me your number last week I had the forethought to put it in my landlines phone book so that's what I'm ringing from."

"Oh right, yes, that was a good idea. It's ok, I figured there was a plausible explanation."

"I take it there's no change with your brother."

"No, I actually thought you were the nurse ringing to tell me he'd woken up."

"Oh ok, well I best get off and free up the line then. I'll stay here until the damn phone has done charging and get some much-needed cleaning done. I'll ring back in a couple of hours and check in again. Do you need anything bringing when the phones done?"

"Erm no, I'm good thanks. Speak to you soon, bye."

"Bye princess."

Ok so he wasn't the jerk face I had made him out to be, so sue me.

Chapter 3

I decided that a walk around the hospital would pass some time. Choosing to walk down the steps instead of taking the lift meant I got to walk off that huge dinner after all. What is it they say 'a moment on the lips, a lifetime on the hips', and in my family that was definitely true. I only have to look at a slice of chocolate cake and I gain weight.

My sister, however, the lucky cow, can eat anything that she wants and not put on a single ounce. It's sickening. We don't get along, not like me and Michael do. I put it down to her coming from mum's first marriage while Michael and I are from her second. Not that either marriage lasted long. Both husbands filed for divorce citing irreconcilable differences, basically our mother's a bitch.

Growing up me and Michael were inseparable, us against the world. Zoey on the other hand was always out with her friends, getting up to goodness knows what. She was mum's angel. She couldn't do anything wrong as far as mum was concerned.

Michael however was painted as the black sheep of the family, always getting the blame for things, even stuff he hadn't done. The final straw for us was his sixteenth birthday. Mum wouldn't allow him to go out but had consented to allowing him one friend over to play video games and even bought them a pizza. Zoey went out to the pub with her boyfriend, when she got home she started mouthing off at Michael; trying to get him to raise his voice just to get him in trouble with Mum.

She did stuff like that all the time, he couldn't hear her though, he was wearing the ear buds I'd bought him for his birthday. She became so irate with him she lost her balance and put her hand out to steady herself with the sideboard but misjudged where she was and instead of leaning on the unit, she ended up putting her hand on the silver serving tray we had our grandmother's crystal vase on.

The tray tipped and the vase smashed on the floor. Mum heard the commotion, at that point Michael chose to take out his ear buds and was extremely confused by what was going on. Zoey had turned on the water works; the usual crocodile tears to get out of everything she did wrong. Mum was going ballistic, that's when Zoey played her hand, blaming Michael for what had happened. Saying he had gotten in her face about coming home bladdered; claiming she was scared he was going to hit her.

How she fell back into the sideboard and that's how the vase broke. Of course, Mum believed every word that came out of Zoey's lying, vindictive mouth. Michael had had enough by that point, he grabbed his phone, coat and games console and went upstairs mumbling about how perfect Zoey gets away with everything. Mum was shouting after him saying she'd had enough of his insolent behaviour and how he's the reason she has a heart condition. She doesn't have a heart condition though, she has heart burn and acid reflux issues due to her crappy diet and poor lifestyle choices. She was still mouthing off at him when he came down with his rucksack and duffel bag. He went through to the conservatory, got his bike, and left. A few mins later he sent me a text.

If the bitch wants to know where I've gone tell her I've gone to Freddie's, I'll call you when I'm settled somewhere, love you M xx

DJ DREAMBOAT

I'd sent a reply telling to be safe and to call me if he needed anything. In reality he'd moved in with dad and Claire our step mum. She was great, the total opposite of Mum. I would have gone with him, but they only had a three-bedroom semi-detached and with the baby due, there was only room enough for one of us. Things didn't get any better after he left, if anything they got worse, but at least I didn't have to endure it for too long.

A year later I moved out. Mum and Zoey were happy at last. They got what they'd wanted since the divorce, just the two of them. With me and Michael out the way for good. And me? I had my own place, a decent sized two bed flat above the local Chinese takeaway.

When Michael turned eighteen he came to live with me, it was like old times but better. We didn't have anything to do with either Mum or Zoey until our dad passed away. Even at the funeral we never spoke, and we didn't go to the wake afterwards. Instead we went back to dad's with Claire and our half-brother, Thomas, where we watched all of dad's favourite movies and ate all his favourite foods. I think he would have liked that.

It wasn't long after that when Michael went backpacking around America and fell in love with a legal secretary. He stayed over there, they got married and had a couple of kids. I adore my niece and nephew but rarely see them. The marriage didn't last and he moved back home and got his own place with three bedrooms so the kids could come stay during the school holidays.

'PING.'

I looked at my phone, it was a text I guessed it was from James, however, it was from my niece, Corrin.

Hey, Aunt Ange, have you heard from dad? He was supposed to facetime me at lunch and he never rang, love C xx

Shit! What should I tell her? I couldn't tell her via text, I'd have to speak to her.

Hey babes, need you to call me A.S.A.P. It's about your dad love A xx

Less than a minute later my phone was ringing. Here goes nothing.

"Hey, C."

"Hey, what's up with dad? What was that noise? Are you in the hospital? Wait is dad in the hospital?"

"C, calm down. I need you to listen. There was an accident. Your dad's had to have major surgery. Honey, they've had to amputate his legs above the knees."

"Oh my God. I, I need to tell Mitchell, will you let me know of any developments. We'll be on the first flight out."

"Yeah sure, love you."

"Love you, too."

Well that went better than I expected. Although the nurse hadn't rung me, I decided to go back to the ward.

My timing was perfect, just as I walked through the double doors, the nurse called me over to tell me Michael had woken up but was still groggy from the anaesthetic and would probably not make a whole lot of sense. I joked that there wouldn't be much change then, we both laughed at the lame joke.

She led me into a side room and I steeled myself. Hooked up to an I.V drip and a heart monitor, he looked so fragile and helpless. The tears flooded my eyes and I collapsed. Next thing I knew I was in the armchair next to Michaels bed, pillow behind my head and one of those awful hospital blankets over my legs. I heard voices but couldn't make out who's they were or where they were coming from.

"Hey, I think she's waking up."

"I'll get her some ice water."

"Thank you."

I opened my eyes to find James hovering over me, all tired and dishevelled.

"Hey there, princess. Welcome back to the land of the living."

"James? What are you doing here? And why am I in a chair?" I tried to stand up but my body wasn't cooperating.

"Easy there, you took quite the tumble."

"How long have I been out for?"

"Three hours, I got here an hour ago. Your niece rang. They will be here tomorrow morning. I told them they can stay at my place and to call at the hospital straight from the airport, so they can see you both before I take them to mine in the van."

"You didn't have to do that; you hardly know me. This is my mess, there's no need to get involved, we don't owe each other anything. We had an amazing weekend together, but now it's back to reality."

"My brother is going to need some serious aftercare, physio, rehabilitation, and possibly prosthetics. There's no need for you to get yourself messed up in all of that. It wouldn't be fair of me to expect you to get involved."

"Woah slow your roll, princess. First of all, yes it was a magical weekend. Second, I have no idea where you live so I can't take them there and third. I offered my place because the nearest hotel is ten miles away and my place is twenty minutes in the van, so don't flatter yourself, ok?"

"I'm sorry James. I-."

"It's ok, I get it, you're emotional. Your brother will probably be in a wheelchair for the rest of his life, and there's me acting like a knight in shining D.J van. I get it, look if it will make you feel better about everything, if it will make you feel better, why don't you give your family your keys and directions to your place? That way, I can take them there."

"Thank you that does make me feel a little better."

"Miss Marsh, here, drink this; then we can talk about your brother and what happens next."

"What is it?"

"Ice water, come on now."

"Oh, ok, thank you."

"I'll go get the doctor."

"Can you not tell me?"

"It's best you hear it from the doctor."

I still wasn't sure exactly what had happened, the last thing I remembered I was being led into the room and seeing Michael all hooked up. I guess I must have passed out from shock. I'm still not sure what if anything James' agender is; only time will tell I guess. My main concern has to be Michael right now, I could hear the nurse talking to the doctor as they came through the door.

I started to get up, but the doctor motioned at me to stay seated. To be honest I don't think I could have stood up, let alone stood up long enough to have a conversation with anyone.

"Well, Miss Marsh."

"Please, call me Angela."

"Very well, Angela. We have some good news. Your brother has been fully conscious and talking for the last hour; and is already complaining about you stealing his spotlight."

"Typical Michael. Where is he? I don't see him."

"That's the other good news we have. Because he's regained consciousness so quickly, we were able to move him onto the main ward. You may go see him once you have eaten and rested. No arguments."

"You won't get any arguments from me on that score doctor. I feel like I've ran a marathon on an empty stomach."

"When was the last time you ate a decent meal?"

"Well, I had cottage pie, chips and gravy followed by jam roley poley and custard just before I came back to the ward, when did you say that was again?"

"You've been out cold for three hours and given it would take ten minutes to come down in the lift-"

"Actually, I walked down the stairs, needed to get my steps in."

"Fine, make that twenty minutes from the canteen to here then, we are talking roughly three and a half hours since you have consumed anything to eat; add to that the affect the shock will have had on your system, no wonder you are running on empty."

James' phone rang and he went out of the room to answer it. I paid it no mind, it wasn't any of my business where he went or who he talks to. I had to stay focused on Michael and his recovery. His place wouldn't be suitable for him to go back to and he would need someone with him twenty-four-seven.

He would also need a nurse and to start with home physio visits. I made up my mind there and then I would move into his place. We would have to turn his downstairs man-cave into a temporary bedroom for him to free up one of the bedrooms for a live-in nurse maybe. Though my place would be better for him.

He always teased me when we were kids for thinking too far ahead, always preparing for the worst yet hoping for the best. I suppose in a way I have been preparing my whole life for this moment. I was so wrapped up in my thoughts

I didn't see or hear James come back in until he touched my arm to grab my attention.

"Hey princess, you were away with the fairies. What were you thinking about?"

"Michael and his aftercare."

"Well speaking of Michael, that was his daughter on the phone. They've just got to the airport and will be taking off soon."

"Thank you again for helping out, you really don't have to."

"And as I keep saying, it's not a problem."

I looked at him standing there with a smirk plastered over his face, I knew he was winding me up and in an odd mixed-up way it was helping. The problem I had wasn't that I didn't want his help, it was that I didn't want to get used to his help and then find I couldn't function without him. The last thing I needed was to get attached and then him disappear. The only thing to do would be to give the twins the key to my place and directions when they arrive, so he can take them there and then his involvement would be over.

Chapter 4

The next morning rolled round. James was back at his place and I was again snoozing in a chair. This one however, was next to Michaels bed. I was hunched over the side of the bed, holding his hand, and drooling all over the blankets. Not a pretty site I can tell you. The twins wouldn't be there for hours yet and James had gone home to shower, eat and sleep.

What I wouldn't give right now for a shower and a hot meal the nurse said I was welcome to use the bathroom on the ward, but I needed my own shower, in my own home. There was no chance of that however, until the twins arrived to stay with their dad.

"Hey Aunty Ange."

Sitting up I wiped the drool from my chin and was given the biggest bear hug from them both. After a couple of minutes, they released me and I was able to catch my breath.

"Hi, you two. How was the flight?"

"Long. This one snored the whole flight."

I giggled as Corrin poked her brother in the ribs.

"Hey, it's not my fault the air pressure affects my sinuses."

"Yeah right, ok, we believe you; thousands wouldn't."

All three of us were creasing ourselves with laughter. The nurse came in and gave us a stern look. It felt like we were in the school playground being reprimanded by the dinner lady. The twins found a couple of smaller chairs and sat at the other side of their dad's bed. Michael was fast asleep, the effects of the pain medication he was on.

I looked across at them, they were my whole world. I missed a lot of the twins' lives, their mother kept them in the states after the divorce; it's easier now they're grown, they can fly over on their own and visit me and their dad as often as work allowed.

They also video chat with him every week. Michael's a great dad. He was always there for them growing up, despite the ocean between them; he never missed the big events. Always flew back for their birthdays, and had a holiday over there when they graduated. I was gutted I missed that but we all had a party at the local hotel the next time they came over to visit and there were tons of photos on social media.

"So, what happens now?"

That was so like Mitchell, straight to the point, no messing around. He was always the same even as a small child; take charge attitude, the first to walk, talk and ride a bike. I always said that he's been here before, definitely not his first time on the hamster wheel of life.

What was it our nan always said? Oh yeah, 'he's a warm en, got an old ed on young shoulders', proper Yorkshire nan was. She taught me and Michael how to bake and knit. We were at hers more often than we were at home. She always took our side against Mum and Zoey, it's been years now since she passed and I think about her every day. Other than school, nans was our safe space away from all the agro at home.

"The doctor will be doing his rounds just after shift change; so we've a good few hours left yet, I was hoping to go home and have a proper shower and something to eat now you guys are here; thought it would give the two of you some alone time with your Dad and then when the doctor's been and we know more; I can give you the keys to my place, my friend James has offered to take you there. Slight change to the plan I know you discussed with him C, but I would feel better having you at my place, hope you don't mind?"

"Not at all, I only agreed to his suggestion of crashing at his place because I was tired and didn't want to argue with him. He can be quite persuasive."

"Oh, trust me, I know."

"So, are you two a thing? How do you know him?"

"No, well, I don't know if you'd call us a thing; we met las week through his job."

"And you've already slept with him? Aunty A you vixen, you must tell me all about it tonight."

"Ok, I think I've got ice cream and wine at home. I'll check when I go back to freshen up. I can order us a pizza or a Chinese if you want, I'm sure you'll be hungry."

"Starved, right, you get off home. We'll see you back here later. Is James going to come pick you up? Or are you going to get a taxi? I didn't see your car in the carpark."

"I hadn't thought about it. Hang on, I'll ring him."

I pulled my phone out my bag and dialled his number, I didn't expect him to answer the phone and I was ready to leave him a voicemail but he answered on the third ring.

"Hey, princess, what's up? Have the kids got there yet?"

"Hi James, yeah they arrived ok, I was wondering if it's not too much trouble could you swing by and pick me up? I really need a shower and a change of clothes. I don't want to put you out or anything."

"Nonsense princess, anything for you, ya know that. Give me five mins and I'll set off, see you soon."

"Thanks, see you soon."

Hanging up I put my phone back in my bag.

"So, princess, is it? And you say you're not a thing, come on pull the other one Aunty Ange."

"You heard that? Oh, dear."

"Oh, dear indeed. I can't wait to meet him."

Half an hour later I felt a gentle kiss on the back of my neck, a tingle ran all the way down my spine. I tried my best to hide the effect he had on me. Clearly, I didn't do a good enough job judging by the look on Corrin's face.

"Hey princess."

"Hi, this is Corrin and Mitchell."

"Hi guys, how was the flight? Get here ok?"

"Yes thanks, so tell us, how did you meet our aunt?"

"She came to one of my parties last week and we hit it off. We hooked up on Saturday, and we've been inseparable since, well apart from last night. I had to go home do single man stuff, the housework won't do itself, after all."

"Oh, Aunt Angela, you finally got one that's house trained."

"Corrin!"

"Ha-ha, it's ok, princess, I'm not offended. It's cute that they look out for you. You ready to go?"

"Yeah thanks, see you later C. If Michael wakes up while I'm gone, tell him I'll be back later."

"Have fun you two, don't do anything I wouldn't do."

Chuckling to myself, I picked up my handbag, gave the twins a hug and placed a kiss on Michael's forehead. I didn't like leaving him, but the twins were there now so I knew he had family with him. I didn't want him to be alone, silly I know but if anything were to happen to him, I wanted him to be with family.

The drive to my place was spent in an awkward silence, I gave James the directions before we got in the van. I just wanted some peace and quiet after the continuous beeping from the machines in the hospital and the buzzing of the fluorescent lights. I was beginning to get a migraine. I needed my shower, my herbal pain meds, and a nanna nap.

DJ DREAMBOAT

"Your castle awaits princess."

"Thank you for bringing me home, and all your help over the last couple of days, I really appreciate it."

"As I keep saying, you're welcome. Really I mean it if there's anything you need, any time, just call me; speaking of, do you want me to hang out and take you back to the hospital later?"

"No, it's ok. I'm going to have a shower and a nap, you best get off home; I'm sure you have things that you need to do."

"Well I do have this weekend's party to get ready for, will you be able to make it? It'll do you good to let your hair down; you've had a stressful couple of days."

"No, Michael needs me. I'll mention it to the twins though, they might like to go."

"Sure thing princess, sweet dreams."

I watched as he drove off the end of the street, certain I wouldn't see him again; unsure how I felt about that, I wondered why it would bother me so much if I didn't. The house was dark and smelt fusty after being shut up since Saturday afternoon. I opened all the downstairs windows and put the kettle on. Sorted out my bathrobe and hung it in the wet room. I loved my bathroom because it was downstairs, I'd bought the ex-council house five years ago when I split from my ex and needed a fresh start.

I chose it because of its location and that it was one of the few detached houses that the council had built in the early 2000's. Although I loved the house, the layout was completely wrong for me, so I hired a local builder and did a complete re model starting with the kitchen, downstairs toilet, and pantry. I bricked up the side door to the kitchen and knocked the kitchen wall down moving it inwards by three feet giving me more space for the wet room and separate laundry room.

What space was lost in the kitchen was made up for with the extension I put on the back of the house. Enabling me to open up the existing space by knocking the kitchen slash living room wall down, creating an open plan room. All the downstairs was wheelchair accessible good thing really, with Michael more than likely being wheelchair bound for life. having the open plan and wet room would be just what he needed. The other side of the house had the attached garage, at the moment it was a junk room.

It was supposed to be my home gym but I never did get around to sorting it; the only things I would need to do would be to make the doorway from the garage into the house, wide enough to fit a wheelchair or powerchair through. Convert the shutter on the front to a wall with low level window and wide framed doorway giving Michael complete freedom and his independence. Leaving the two spare bedrooms upstairs for the twins when they come to visit.

The only thing I needed to do was convince Michael my place was better suited to his recovery than his. I decided to call the builder first thing in the morning and get him to come over and measure up for the work I would need doing.

Chapter 5

My phone woke me up from the most restful sleep I'd had in days. Picking it up I noticed James's name on the caller ID, I nearly didn't answer but then I noticed the time.

"What is it? What's happened?"

"Michael's awake and asking for you. I'm on my way to pick you up make sure you're ready. I'll be there in ten minutes."

He hung up, no 'hi princess, bye princess,' he even sounded a bit agitated. It didn't take me long to get ready. I'd laid out my clothes on my ottoman at the bottom of my bed before I went in the shower. After I was dressed in my *G.N.R* t-shirt and black leggings, I brushed my hair and put it in a messy bun, letting the fine, straggling auburn hairs fall where they wanted. Normally, I would slick them back and spray them down, but I neither had the time nor the inclination.

True to his word, James was here on time. He'd ditched his staple Hawaiian shirt for a baggy tee, washed out denim jeans and converse trainers. Damn he looked hot. Checking myself I walked towards the van, trying to avoid eye contact. If I saw those bedroom eyes, that's where we'd end up and I needed to be at the hospital, Michael needed me!

"Hi, thanks for picking me up."

"Hey, you ready? Good come on get in."

"Yeah ok, let me lock up."

As the lock clicked into place I made up my mind to find out what was going on with him. I climbed into the passenger side, fastened my seatbelt, and sighed

"That was a heavy sigh."

"James, I don't know what's going on, or what I've done wrong, but this whole change of attitude towards me, is creeping me out."

He fidgeted with the hem of his t-shirt, mumbling his reply.

"It's nothing you've said or done, or not said or not done. It's a me problem, not a you problem. It'll be ok; just got some stuff I need to figure out, and a problem I need to find the solution to."

"Why didn't you just talk to me? Instead of bottling things up.

"Reaching over, I placed my hand on his knee. He raised his head to talk to me.

"Like I said, it's a me problem, not a you problem. Plus, you know what men are like. We don't talk about all the emotional stuff. It's not our thing. I'm also not used to having someone, to share things with."

"You've never had friends you could bro talk to?"

"Yeah, of course I have. I meant no one special. You know, like you."

"I'm nothing special, just plain boring Angela."

"Princess, nothing about you is plain or boring."

"Oh, so it's princess again is it? Make up your mind god damn it."

"Sorry I let my problems affect us. I'll do better from now on princess."

Leaning over me, I could smell his cologne. Damn it he smelled so good. Keeping my distance from him was going to be hard. I felt his soft warm lips gently press against mine and I was gone, all thoughts of keeping my distance faded in an instant, he knew my buttons and how to push them. Boy did he know how, all thoughts of Michael disappeared.

"Maybe we should take this inside princess?"

"I need to be at the hospital."

"Are you sure you can't spare an hour?"

"Well, I suppose I could ring Corrin and see how the land lies with Michael."

"Sounds like a plan. I need you to know, I've never done anything like this before. It isn't just a fling for me princess."

"Neither have I."

I fumbled though my bag for my phone, dialled Corrin and waited for her to answer. She didn't. I shot James a worried glance and was about to send her a text when she rang me back.

"Hey Aunty, sorry I couldn't get to the phone, I was talking to the nurse."

"Hey, C, is everything ok? Why were you talking to the nurse?"

"Just girl stuff. M's gone to get us a *KFC* and dad's sleeping."

"Again. He got bored waiting for you."

"So, there's no rush to come back?"

"Nope, no rush, take your time. doc's not been round yet."

"Ok, thanks, C. See you later."

"Have fun and tell James I said hi."

I turned off my mobile and put it back in my bag, gave him a sideways glance and smiled. That was all the green light he needed, leaning over me again he took my chin in his hand and brought my mouth to his. The kiss was deep and sensual. I was his to command and he knew it. Closing the front door behind me, he spun me round to face him, his eye's locked on me with a sexual hunger. I pulled off his t-shirt revealing his abs, his chest was just as glorious as

I remembered. stood before me This Adonis of a man was mine to devour, and devour him I would, every seductive inch of him. I reached for his belt only to find he was already unfastening it. I gently slid my hand down to find him erect and standing to attention like a good soldier. As he slid his hands up my ribs lifting my t shirt as his fingers caressed my skin, I felt like *Baby* from *Dirty Dancing*. My head was spinning.

His kiss was deep and seductive, filled with a need, a need I reciprocated. My leggings were the next to be discarded, he slid his hand into my pants and found me wet and wanton, a hooked finger found its way to the sweet spot and I was putty in his hands. Sensing I wasn't able to walk anywhere he scooped me into his muscular arms and carried me upstairs.

My bedroom door was still wide open from earlier. Carrying me with no effort at all, he walked towards my bed and placed me on it. He stood looking at me as if painting a picture of me in his mind for re-runs later on. I couldn't blame him after all, I was doing the same thing.

Lying next to me on the bed, tracing the contours of my breasts with his fingers, he unclasped my bra with ease and threw it across the room. Placing my breast in his mouth he sucked on my nipple teasing me with his tongue as his hands caressed and devoured the rest of my body. I was in total ecstasy. Another glorious hour later, we were dressed and on the way to the hospital.

Chapter 6

Michael was sat up in bed chatting to both the twins when we got there, he almost looked like himself; from the waist up at least. Corrin was the first to spot me. As I sat with them she waved to James, and I turned to see him standing awkwardly in the doorway. I could tell he wasn't sure if he was welcome or not. Waving him over I spoke to him.

"Don't just stand there like a dilly drip, come on in and sit down. He won't bite."

Still unsure, James edged slowly into the ward. Michael smiled and waved him over to sit with us; this seemed to be the welcome he was waiting for and he came to sit with us.

"Michael, this is James, he's my..."

Corrin chuckled at my hesitation to finish the sentence.

"He's her fancy man, that's what he is."

"Corrin! Behave."

Everyone laughed and just like that any apprehension we felt disappeared.

"Hi Michael, it's nice to meet you. How ya feeling? Apart from the obvious."

"Can't complain I suppose. I'm still alive, that's the main thing. So, I've lost my legs, things could have been a lot worse."

"That's a real mature way to look at things. I know I'd be freaking out if it was me."

"No point crying over spilt milk, what's done is done. I've got to focus on my recovery and how my future looks legless."

"You should sue the company and the driver, dad."

"It doesn't work like that over here Mitchell. Besides, we don't know the situation, why the driver did what he did. He could have a family, kids of his own. I'm not going to sue the company; the poor blokes probably already lost his job because of the accident; unless it was mechanical failure in the truck then he should be ok. No use speculating though, we'll know more when the police finish their investigation. That reminds me Ange, the cops came by while you were... well anyway. They came for my statement and their reviewing the cctv from the motorway cameras, so we should know soon what happened."

"If it is vehicle fault, surely you could then sue the company? And the other driver in the car that crashed into you could, too. There's got to be some way of getting some compensation from them. It can't be too different to how it is back home, dad."

The nurse popped her head into the ward doorway and brought us out of the conversation.

"Right guys it's kicking out time I'm afraid. He needs his sleep, you can come back tomorrow."

We all said our goodbye's to Michael and left him to sleep. James walked with the twins off the ward while I stayed behind to have a chat with the nurse.

"Hi, I missed the doctor tonight. I was wondering if the he was going to be around during visiting hours tomorrow? I have"

"a couple of questions I need to run by him."

"Well there's shift change at 8:00 a.m. and 8:00 p.m. so the doctor will be around for one of those I think he's on the night shift tomorrow. Hang on while I check the system for you."

"Thank you."

James came back wondering where I was. After I explained I'd only be a few minutes, he waited with me, saying he didn't want me out in the dark this late on my own. That made me giggle. He was so chivalrous and old fashioned; it was sweet but totally unnecessary.

"Angela!"

"Yeah?"

"I've checked and Dr Green is on nights tomorrow, so he'll be here for shift change at 8:00 p.m. I'm guessing you will be here for the entirety of visiting hours?"

"The twins will be here during the day. I'll be at work, so I'll come straight here after my shift's over."

"Ok, I'll let the day shift know to expect them and put a note on the system for Dr Green that you want to speak with him before he begins his rounds."

"That's wonderful, thank you."

"So, princess I was thinking. I won't be able to fit all three of you in the van so, I'll pay for a taxi for the three of you to go back to your place. I can pick up the twins, bring them here tomorrow then I can take them for something to eat and drop them at yours afterwards when you get here. I doubt they'll be cleared to drive your car, will they?"

"Actually, they are, because of Michael they have dual citizenship, including both British passports and British driving licences. They'll be able to drive down in my car using the sat nav and I'll get a taxi straight from work. It was nice of you to offer though. What would I do without you? My knight in Hawaiian shirts."

"Well let's hope we never have to find out."

"That sounded ominous. Does it have anything to do with why you've been distant?"

"Yeah, I-,"

"Come on we talked about this already. You can tell me.

You've done so much for me and my family, let me do this for you."

"Ok but not here, I'll swing by your place later. There is something I need to do first. Want me to pick up a Chinese on my way over?"

"No, it's ok, the twins want a pizza so I'll order one in. I can order an extra one if you fancy that instead."

"Yeah that would be great. Double peperoni with pineapple and jalapeno please."

"Ok strange combination. Don't be expecting any lovin after unless you brush your teeth first."

"What if I leave off the jalapeno? Do I get some lovin then?"

"Absolutely not."

"Ah so it's the pineapple you object to. I see your one of those."

I laughed. He had a way with his words, that always managed to get through whatever emotional blockage I had going on.

"I'm sure I have no idea what you're talking about."

We walked outside and found the twins waiting for us outside the entrance.

"Took you two long enough, what were you up to?"

"Get your mind out of the gutter Corrin. I was talking to the nurse, arranging a chat with the doctor tomorrow to talk about your dad and what happens next. But enough of that now."

"Here's my phone book a taxi back to mine and we can get those pizzas ordered you wanted."

James said his goodbyes to Mitchell and waved to Corrin. Flooring me with a lingering kiss before getting in his van and driving off, leaving me with the twins to wait for the taxi. When I got home, I got the usual Spanish inquisition off Corrin. After I showed them to their rooms, I got the table ready for when the pizza's arrived, and ran myself a hot bubble bath, leaving Mitchell with the money to pay for the food.

Half an hour later I was in my PJs and opening a bottle of wine. The pizzas arrived about ten minutes before James did and the twins made room for him at the table so he could sit next to me. I got the distinct impression throughout the meal that they were playing matchmaker; quizzing him about his interests, work, and family. The whole kit and kaboodle.

I felt sorry for him but he was loving it, and for the first time that day I saw him truly relax. I wasn't going to push him into telling me what got him so upset, he'd tell me in his own time. The twins cleared away the pizza boxes and James offered to wash the glasses, leaving me the rare opportunity to relax and put my feet up. As I sat on the sofa looking at him busying himself in the kitchen, I realised I was falling for him.

I was never one for believing in love at first sight, but this was as close to it as I had ever been. This man made me feel things I thought I would never feel. Confident, sexy, amazing. I only hoped that my feelings were reciprocated in some way. For the first time in my life I could see a future with someone.

"We're going to head up to bed Aunty Ange, you two kids have fun now."

I picked up the oven gloves and threw them at her; she laughed it off and they went up to their rooms. James came and sat with me on the sofa lifted my legs, placed them across his lap and started rubbing the soles of my feet. It was heaven. We were already acting like we'd been a couple for months not days. I looked at him, he smiled that cheeky grin and I was lost and I didn't care.

"So, you see the thing is, when I got home earlier there was a voicemail on my office answering machine."

"Oh, so we're talking about this now?"

"Yeah, I'm afraid if I don't tell you now I will lose my nerve."

"Take your time."

"The voicemail was from the family solicitor."

"Sounds serious, what's happened?"

"It is. My father passed away on Saturday and I have to be at the will reading on Wednesday."

"Oh, James! I'm so sorry. Were you and your dad close?"

"Yeah, after mum died it was just the two of us. He was a nightclub DJ and when he couldn't get a sitter he'd take me along to his gig's. That's how I got into the music scene, he retired ten years ago and moved to Scotland, married a feisty Scottish lass half his age and my half-brother was born a year later. I've never seen him."

"Scotland? Wow that's a fair trek. Wait, that means you'll have to set off tomorrow."

"Yeah, I'll have to leave 9:00 p.m. at the latest. I didn't want to leave without saying goodbye."

"Do you know how long you'll need to be there?"

"Not a clue. I suppose it all depends on what it says in the will."

I sat quietly taking it all in. I wasn't sure what this would mean for us.

"Listen, it's getting late and I need to drive back. I should go."

"You can't drive, you've had two glasses of wine. You could stay here, I'll make up the couch."

"The couch! Why can't I sleep in your room princess?"

"Because. I have work in the morning and if you sleep in my room, I won't get any sleep."

"Fair enough princess, I get that. Sweet dreams."

"You too."

"Always do when I dream of you princess."

He winked at me and kissed my cheek, gently placing my feet back on the floor. I told him where the wet room was and that he was welcome to shower before bed if he wished. After handing him the spare blankets and pillow from the cupboard I went to bed. But I couldn't sleep. The thought of him being downstairs made me restless. After tossing and turning for about an hour I saw the clock turn midnight. Fed up I snuck downstairs to make a drink. Maybe a hot chocolate would help me sleep, I doubted it but it was worth a try.

I'd have to be as quiet as I could, mainly so I didn't wake the twins. Corrin was a light sleeper like Michael. Mitchell, however, could sleep through a freight train going past the house just like me and his mother. Plus, there was my prince charming sleeping on the sofa. If I woke him up I would definitely not get to sleep.

Being careful to avoid the creaking top step, I made my way downstairs and into the kitchen. I needn't have worried about waking him, he was fast asleep splayed out like a snoring starfish. It was quite cute really. I decided to boil the milk in a pan on the cooker rather than in the microwave as I usually did. Even though he was fast on. I didn't want to wake him.

The milk came to the boil and I took the pan off the cooker, placing it on the heat proof mat on the kitchen side while I got the Ovaltine and the chocolate shavings out of the cupboard. I was placing the pan back down. After pouring the milk into my mug, as I replaced the pan to the stove I felt a pair of hands snake around my waist and warm soft lips kiss the back of my neck.

"Well hello there, princess. Thought you were in bed fast asleep; dreaming of your prince charming."

"Couldn't sleep. There's this random weirdo sleeping on my sofa that's got the hots for me."

"Oh, so I'm a weirdo, am I? I'll show you weird. Come here, you Vixen you."

He spun me round to face him and kissed me with a deep feverish passion. This was not going to be a night for sleep, and I doubted I would be able to walk properly in the morning, but I didn't care. I had to make the most of the time we had left before he went to Scotland.

Chapter 7

As I predicted I didn't get any sleep at all. I did however discover things about my body and James that I wasn't expecting; the man was a stallion in the bedroom and knew all the right moves to get me singing in ecstasy. Under different circumstances I would have gone to Scotland with him, but I needed to stay here and look after Michael.

The twins can't stay here indefinitely, they have their jobs and friends back in the states. Michael is my responsibility now, and as fun as this was with James I knew deep down it couldn't last. He was off to Scotland for goodness knows how long and I had to become nurse and goodness knows what else to Michael for at least six months.

I made the decision then to tell James to stay in Scotland as long as they needed him to, and to not worry about me. He would find someone new, someone who came without baggage and complicated relatives. I slipped out of bed and ran myself a warm bath; it was 6:00 a.m. and I had to leave for work in an hour. I couldn't exactly go into work smelling like a hooker after a night on the job.

While my bath was running I made a pot of coffee, put my favourite seeded bread in the toaster, grabbed a banana out of the fruit bowl and got the chocolate spread out the cupboard. I was going to need my energy after the night I'd had. With my toast in one hand and coffee in the other, I went back upstairs and got to the bathroom just in time to stop the bath from overflowing. Placing my coffee on the sideboard in my room and shoving the last piece of toast in my mouth, I climbed in the bath and took a few minutes to relax before the regime of washing my hair and scrubbing my body began.

James strolled into the bathroom just as I was rinsing the conditioner out of my hair. Ignoring him I carried on with the task in hand, totally oblivious to the fact that he was now stood next to the bath. As I glanced upwards in between rinses, I found him staring at me with lust in his eyes.

"Woah there, cowboy, slow your role. I've got to leave for work at seven and you've got to go home and pack for Scotland. We are not having a repeat of last night, now go and get dressed so I can finish my bath in peace."

"Can't a man admire the beauty of the Goddess before him without being accused of wanting what he wants?"

"No, not when that man is you and you're looking at me the way you are doing. Now go, go on. I mean it get dressed. The twins will be up soon and I need to finish in here before they get up."

"Yes ma'am!"

He turned and walked out the bathroom with a swagger giggling to myself I finished up in the bath and walked out just as Corrin was stumbling out of her room. She was definitely not a morning person. I could hear the guys talking downstairs about sports and how football is better than American football; they'd be at it for ages, giving me time to get ready for work in peace.

Corrin opened my door and sat on the bottom of my bed, giving me the 'I know what you were up to last night' look. I knew what she wanted, so after I put my hair up in a high ponytail I spun round on my vanity stool and braced myself for the questions.

"Soo, you had fun last night. No need to spill I heard it all."

I went bright red with embarrassment.

"Oh crap, C, I'm so sorry. Living on my own I forget how thin the walls are sometimes."

"No apology needed, I'm just glad you're finally getting some action, it's about time. How long's it been since you and Richard split? Two three years? It doesn't do a girl any good to go without the fun things in life."

"Corrin!"

"What? You know I'm right, we need a girly day while I'm here, shopping, Mani Pedi, the works."

"I can't Corrin, I've got work today."

"Tomorrow then. We can leave Mitchell with dad, they can catch up on man things like sport and women."

I shot her the mum look and she just giggled.

"Fine, it's my day off tomorrow, so yeah, we've not had a girly day in years. I've got to head off to work soon but I'm leaving you the car so you can both go to the hospital, I'll get James to take me to work and get a taxi from there to the hospital. See you later."

I left her to do whatever she needed to and went downstairs to make a flask of coffee and make my pack up for work. The guys were outside at the van, it looked like James was showing Mitchell his DJ equipment in the back. I waved to them through the window before going out to join them.

Mitchell went back inside, not one for his subtlety, which left me alone with James yet again. This was becoming a habit of theirs; leaving me on my own with him and while I appreciate their efforts they were not aware of his impending trip to Scotland.

"Hi princess, you all clean and ready for work?"

"Yeah about that, I need to ask you a favour. Would you be able to drop me off at work please?"

DJ DREAMBOAT

"Yeah sure no problem. Just tell me where and hop on in."

We travelled in silence. I let him concentrate on his driving while I contemplated my future without him in it.

"Right then princess you're here. That'll cost a tumble in the sheets before I go to Scotland later."

He winked at me, I leaned over to give him a kiss before getting out of the van. The last place I wanted to be was work right now, but what choice did I have?

"Hey prince charming, you wanna come in for a coffee before I start my shift?"

"Yeah ok, you sure your boss won't mind?"

"Yep, absolutely sure. I am the boss."

"Soo you could take the day off and not open at all?"

"I could if today wasn't delivery day and I didn't have a kids party in three hours."

"So, what I'm hearing is if I want to spend the day with you, I have a delivery to help unload and a kid's party to get through. That's doable. How old are the kids?"

"It's a tenth birthday party. The delivery should be here in an hour giving me enough time to unpack it and get the place ready before the kids arrive for the party."

"Ok, I'll stay and help, I'm all packed up at home; just need to chuck my bag into the van and drive up there. Ring the parents of the birthday kid and ask them if they want a party upgrade to a free DJ. I've got all the top chart songs on the hard drive and my portable decks in the back of the van. I've found kids tend to behave better if they have something fun to listen to."

"James, you're a genius. I could kiss you."

"Well I'm right here princess, and I'm all yours."

"Until tonight then you go off to Scotland for goodness knows how long."

"Ah don't be like that, princess. I'll only be there till Thursday. Got a gig on Friday night at the university. Some frat boy's birthday and end of exam party."

"Oh, I feel like a right bitch now."

"You didn't think I was leaving for good, did you?"

"Well I didn't know how long you'd be gone for. I did to be honest. I was worried you'd get up there, meet some gorgeous Scottish lass and choose not to come back. I'm not exactly a prize catch, and there's Michael to take into consideration now."

"He'll take up all my spare time."

"Listen, princess, I'm all in. Your problems are now my problems. I thought you knew that? I think the twins are great, and I'm looking forward to getting to know Michael. You've rocked my world. There is no me without you."

"Wow, I, I'm speechless."

"Then I best make the most of the opportunity while I have it, come here and kiss me."

I fell into his arms and kissed him like my life depended on it. To some extent it did. I knew there and then that this man was my salvation and I was falling for him and hard. I could cope without him for three days, well four if you include the uni party he had to gig for. I'm a big girl.

Tomorrow I'll be occupied with a girly day with Corrin and now I had a purpose to what I was shopping and pampering for. I had a man to look my best for. To look after myself for. How had my day flip flopped from one of bleak despair to one of hope?

Chapter 8

9:00 p.m. arrived far too soon for my liking. James decided to come to the hospital with me and stay till he had to leave for Scotland, that way he could say goodbye to us all at once. I knew that he was only going for a few days but it still felt like my heart was being ripped out of my chest when we waved him off from the hospital car park.

"He'll be back on Thursday, and you've got our girly day to look forward to tomorrow."

I knew Corrin was right, and she was doing her best to cheer me up and take my mind off things.

"Do you want a Chinese tonight and a bottle of wine? We could watch *Netflix*, is there anything good on yours? I love that you get different shows to us. My besties back in the States, always ask me about what new shows and films I've watched when I go back home."

"Erm yes to the wine and takeaway, I'm not fussed about *Netflix* at the minute its full of mushy stuff and I need to watch something that's got some blood and guts in it, take my mind off James for a couple of hours."

"There's a new series started on *Disney+* we could watch."

"Cool, if its action then Mitchell will watch it too. I'll drive us back to yours and that way you can phone in the takeaway on route. Order what you want and a beef in black bean sauce for Mitchell and I'll have a Chicken Chow Mein, we can share a portion of chips and prawn crackers."

"Sounds like a plan, if it's going to be the three of us then I best get two bottles of wine and a six pack. What does Mitchell drink nowadays? Lager or beer?"

"He'll drink anything, he's not fussed."

With the evening planned, I phoned in the order while Corrin drove us home via the shop to get the drinks. All the way home Mitchell watched funny cat videos on his phone. An hour later we were all sat watching the TV, enjoying our food and chatting away about anything to keep my mind off the fact that James wasn't here with us.

Midnight rolled around and we all went to bed, it didn't take me long to fall asleep. The next morning, I woke, showered, and got ready. As expected I was the first one up and made a pot of coffee for everyone while I waited for Corrin to wander downstairs. It didn't take long for the smell of the coffee to waft through the house and wake the sleeping twins. Mitchell was the first to emerge from his slumber with

Corrin a few minutes later, rubbing her eyes and bumping into the sofa half drunk on a mixture of alcohol and sleep.

"Morning, sleepy head. You've got twenty minutes to get ready before we leave."

"Huh! Why only twenty minutes?"

"Because I have to call in at work and do a couple of things before we have our girly day."

"Well why can't you go do that while I get ready?"

"I suppose, I could. Mitchell, will you make sure she's ready for when I get back please?"

"Sure thing, I'll ply her with coffee and keep her focused. I can't wait to be rid of the pair of you, be nice to go see dad and it be just the two of us. Would you leave me the car when you get back so I can drive to the hospital? Or do you need it?"

DJ DREAMBOAT

"No, you can have the car we'll take the train into the city and have dinner at the Red Lion. maybe have a couple of glasses of wine."

"Thanks, Aunty Ange."

"Listen you're both grown up now, I think we can drop the aunty, don't you?"

"Are you sure?"

"Absolutely, I was fifteen when my dad's best friend told me to just call him Eric. Now that you're both in your twenties,"

"I think it's overdue. And that's the last I'm saying on the matter. Now I'll get off to work I'll be back in thirty minutes tops, love you both."

"We love you too, Aunty!"

They both giggled and I knew that they were just messing with me. I grabbed my keys from the table and left to go check on the shop. The drive there on my own was great, I put the radio on and my favourite band was playing my favourite song. Cranking up the volume I wound the windows down. The crisp autumn air, the smell of wet fallen leaves and my favourite band blasting out the radio. I was in heaven!

There wasn't much I needed to do at the shop, just check the post and any emails I may have got. I checked the calendar to see what parties I had coming up. Good job I did, there were three booked in over the next fortnight. The first being this Saturday for a group of ten. Searching the emails, I checked for the customers details that booked the party, then double checked the stock. I had to make sure I had what I needed. Thankfully I did. One less thing to worry about. I would, however, need to do a warehouse shop, for the other two parties.

Thinking of the parties, my mind drifted to the last one I had and how James had offered his day to help. The kids had loved it and the parents said it was the best kids party they had been to, that they would pass on the good word about my little shop; and it was all down to James. MY JAMES! I liked the sound of that. Checks done, a quick dust and floor sweep and I was done and ready to go home to collect Corrin and start our much-needed girly day.

Chapter 9

"You ready, C?"

"Yeah just need to grab my purse and we're out of here."

No matter how long I live I will not get used to the American terminology for things. To me a purse is what you put your money in, but in America a bag is called a purse and a purse is called a wallet whether you're a man or a woman. Corrin had picked up some English words as she was growing up, and would lapse into a more English way of speaking, the longer she was staying here visiting her dad, but there were some words that stuck and purse was one of them. It confused me at times.

The first time she picked up a bag and not an actual purse. I questioned her and She laughed at the confusion on my face, and then laughed even harder when she had explained and I still looked like I'd been slapped in the face with a wet fish. Over the years, the confusion over our dialects and terminology has lessened somewhat, but I still giggle to myself when she calls her bag a purse.

"Right, I'm ready Angela. Where are we going first?"

"Well, if Mitchell wouldn't mind dropping us off at the local train station, we can get the 10:15 a.m. train into Manchester, grab some dinner and then hit the shops in the *Trafford centre*"

"Or we could go to Leeds or Sheffield it's up to you."

"Which one is the closest?"

"Sheffield is the closest, the shopping centre there has a *TGI Fridays* and a *5 Guys* or there's *McDonalds* and *KFC* among others to choose from. We could go there first, eat then shop all in one place."

"I like the sound of the Sheffield one, can we go there please."

"No problem, I can top up my *Lush* collection while we're there as well, I'm running low on bath bombs."

"What is *Lush* and why do they sell bath bombs?"

I laughed at her curiosity and confusion.

"It's a shop that sells gorgeous body products that are completely natural, their bath bombs are amazing. They do little ones for kids, too. They also do shampoo bars and shower gels you'll love it."

"Can't wait, can we go there first before we eat?"

"Sure thing, shopping in there always works me up an appetite."

So, the day was planned. Mitchell was to drop us off at the station so we could take the tram to *Meadowhall* and I would show Corrin the wonders of *The Lanes* and everything else the place had to offer. As we'd be there a fair few hours. I left Mitchell some money so he could get something from the hospital canteen and asked him to text me with any developments.

Corrin had never been on the tram before and was really surprised at how quiet and clean it was compared to the tube trains back home. I told her if she liked these, then she'd love our trains. And promised her we could go on a train ride one day before they went back home. Although their leaving date hadn't been discussed I knew they couldn't stay indefinitely. Corrin worked as a freelance photographer and Mitchell was an Architect for a big company in New York. They loved their jobs and their life in the States.

DJ DREAMBOAT

Corrin had talked in the past about relocating to England to be nearer her dad. Maybe this would be the push she needed to make the move across the pond; as for Mitchell he liked the idea of living in England but had never really talked about making a permanent move. But that was a discussion for later.

After a trip to Lush Corrin was extremely relaxed, she had bought one of every bath bomb, and a couple of shampoo bars. We perused the map and Corrin, decided she wanted to try the fish shop in the *Oasis* called *Tasty Plaice*.

I opted for my usual from *KFC* but got my drink from *McDonalds*. We sat in the raised part of the eating area and chatted about all the shops we were going to go to. The first port of call were the lingerie shops, and *Primark*. We decided to break up the shopping to watch a movie in the in-house cinema, opting for a comedy was definitely the best idea.

It was nearly 6:00 p.m. when Mitchell rang to ask if we needed a lift home. I was so happy that we wouldn't have to drag all of our bags back onto the tram, plus with a lift home I would have enough time to have a quick shower and change of clothes before going to the hospital. The last thing I wanted was to be talking to the doctor and smelling like a sweaty bin bag.

"Bloody hell! Is there anything left in the building or did you buy everything?"

"No, Mitchell, we left some for everyone else, I think."

Corrin laughed as I winked at her, we put all our bags in the boot and climbed in the back seat.

"Take us home, Jeeves."

"Right away mi lady."

We all laughed as Mitchell drove out of the carpark, he turned on the radio and we rocked out to some classic 80's tunes all the way home. I left the twins to carry the bags into the house and went straight into the wet room to have my much needed, shower. As I washed my hair I mused over the day and smiled to myself at the little things that had happened. Corrins first bite of a battered sausage, her reaction to seeing someone order fish chips and mushy pees was priceless, then there was her insistence that I buy the skimpiest outfit they had in the lingerie shop.

I opted for a black lace two piece and a matching purple lace kimono chemise. I had never in my life bought anything so transparent or raunchy. Corrin encouraged me by saying James would love it, that his eyes would pop the second he saw me in the ensemble. I reminded her that the plan was to excite him, not kill him. Her reply was that at least he'd die a happy man; so, against my better judgement I bought them along with a couple of other little things and we headed for coffee.

Once showered and dressed Mitchell drove us to the hospital, and the twins sat with Michael while I spoke to the doctor. He gave me some good news and I couldn't wait to share it with them; so as soon as I got back to the ward I pulled them to one side.

"They may be letting Michael home in a week or two if he continues to make the progress he is doing. I know it's late but I'm going to ring my builder friend, who did the alteration to the house and ask him to come around tomorrow to speak with you Mitchell, I'd love you to work your magic on the plans for the garage. That way Dave can get to work a.s.a.p."

"And what if he's busy or he can't get it finished before dad's ready to leave the hospital?"

"Then we will have to make do the best we can or look for any rehab centres, see if they can take him for a couple of weeks till the alterations are done. You go tell your dad the good news. I'm going to ring James and let him know."

"Sounds good to us, let us know if you need any help with the cost. He's our dad after all. Chipping in to help pay for everything is the least we can do."

"That's really kind of you guys, and if I need any help I'll let you know. For now just drawing up the plans with Dave will do, and if you really want to help then getting the shopping in would be great thanks."

They went back into Michael while I pulled out my phone and rang Dave. He picked up on the third ring. We chatted about the situation and he agreed to come by the house first thing. The next phone call was going to be slightly more difficult. I chickened out and sent a text instead.

Hey, you. Got some good news about Michael today, wanted you to be the first to know, ring me when you get the chance xx

I put my phone back in my bag only for it to ring, I assumed it would be Dave wanting to ask me something about tomorrow, but when I looked at the caller I.D, it was James.

"Hi princess."

"Hey you."

"So, what's this good news?"

"Well, Michael is doing great and the doctor said earlier that if he keeps progressing the way he is doing, they might be able to let him come home soon."

"Princess, that's amazing. I bet the twins are excited. Will they let him come home before they have to go back to the states?"

"We haven't discussed when they plan to go back yet. I was going to talk to them about that when we got home from the hospital."

"Look, I've got to get back to the wake. I'll call you tomorrow about teatime. They'll have read the will by then."

"Oh ok, speak to you tomorrow, bye." He hung up without saying goodbye, I guessed he was quite tipsy or the worry of the whole situation relieved him of his manners. It didn't really matter in the grander scheme of things, he would be home on Thursday and we would no doubt see each other at the weekend. In the meantime, I had plenty to keep myself occupied with; between the shop, Michael and the twins, there wasn't any time to be worrying about James and what he was getting up to in Scotland.

I gathered my thoughts, plastered on the realest fake smile I could muster and went back to Michael and the twins. The last thing I needed was the Spanish inquisition. I decided not to tell them I'd spoken to James and just sat down next to Corrin.

"You were gone a while. What did Dave say? Or did you really sneak off to ring lover boy?"

She elbowed me in the ribs and smiled at me, knowing full well I'd spoken to James. She could read me like a book.

"I spoke to Dave and he's coming by first thing tomorrow morning, as for James, I texted him to let him know the good news about Michael and he rang me. We didn't get to chat long, it's no biggy really. I suppose he's busy with everything there, and he'll be back on Thursday so I'll see him soon."

She gave me the mum look and I knew she wasn't going to let it go.

"Ok, spill, what happened?"

"Well, it's just, you know how he always calls me princess? Well, when he was saying goodbye, he..."

"He what?"

"He didn't call me princess. He just said that he'd call me tomorrow, didn't even say goodbye, see ya, nothing. I'm probably just being silly and there's got to be a reasonable explanation for it. He's just buried his dad after all."

"I suppose the formalities of phone calls are the last thing on his mind right now."

"You're not being silly. I don't care how busy he is he should have at least said goodbye."

"I'd rather not talk about it if you don't mind. Let's just sit with your dad and then go home. I'll cook. What do you fancy? bolognaise or pasta bake?"

"Oooo, chicken and bacon pasta bake please. I haven't had your home cooking in years. What about you Mitchell? You want Angela's famous chicken and bacon pasta bake for tea?"

"Sounds good to me, what we washing it down with?"

"That's your department today, I bought the last two lots." We chatted with Michael for about an hour then called at the supermarket on the way home. I wasn't sure if I had everything in that I needed for the meal, so I bought fresh of everything. The twins chose the shape of pasta they wanted and Mitchell bought the alcohol, opting for some mixed fruit cider instead of the usual wine and lager.

It'd been years since I'd had cider and was intrigued by this new one that the supermarket had started selling, but never got around to trying it. By 10:00 p.m. I was cooking and the twins were watching a new show on *Netflix*. I didn't pay attention to the name of it, I left them to it while I cooked.

We opted to sit at the table rather than on the sofa, and turned our phones off so we wouldn't be disturbed. It was the nicest meal I'd had in a long while and the cider was actually really good and went with the meal really well. I would definitely be buying some more next time I did the big shop. Mitchell offered to wash up and Corrin dried the dishes leaving me the opportunity to get an early night. I contemplated turning my phone back on to check my voicemail but decided against it. Instead, turned on my alarm clock radio tuning into the greatest hits station and set my alarm for 7:00 a.m.

It didn't take me long to fall asleep, and the alarm was blaring out at me before I knew it. First on the agenda was a shower then breakfast before Dave came around to take all the measurements and talk shop with Mitchell. As I walked into the kitchen, I could see him on the sofa fast asleep, with plans for the garage on the coffee table.

Bless him, he must have been up all night working on them and just crashed on the sofa, too tired to go up to bed. I sneaked a peak at them and they looked really good, if they became a reality then the garage would be amazing. Breakfast was cereal, I didn't have the time or the energy to make a full English.

Dave arrived while I was washing my bowl and spoon, by this point Mitchell was awake and organising the plans. I sent Dave into him and left them to hash it out between them, they were the ones that had to get it done after all. I was just bank rolling the project.

I'd decided to go into work and keep myself busy, when I got back Dave had gone and Mitchell was on the phone to his boss in the states, he seemed really excited. I figured he would tell me all about it later so I left him to it and made a start on preparing dinner for the three of us. On my way home from work I decided to call at the butchers and buy some mince to make a lasagne with a twist, it's a pretty easy dish, boil the pasta while browning the mince in a separate pan add the lasagne sauce to the mince, drain the pasta when cooked and mix it into the mince and voila, all done.

"Dinner's ready guys, come and get it."

Corrin was the first to the table, she just stood there staring at the food.

"Are you going to just stand there and stare at it or sit down and eat it, C."

"Wow, Angie this looks amazing, what is it?"

"It's my own twist on lasagne, I call it lasagne pasta. Tuck in. Let me know what you think."

They absolutely loved it, cleared their plates, and asked if there was any left over. Unfortunately, there wasn't but I promised to make it for them again before they went back to the states. Corrin made me write down the instructions for her so she could make it herself. I loved cooking for them, I always have done since they were little and used to go visit them before Michael split from their mum.

I have to admit that I was loving having them here, and soon I would soon be able to look after and cook for Michael again, like I did when he lived with me before moving to the states.

Chapter 10

Thursday came sooner than I had expected it to. I woke up early and felt like a flourish of butterflies were trying to escape my stomach. I tried to distract myself with housework but it didn't help, so I decided to walk to work as the twins were using the car today to go see Michael at the hospital. Being alone all day was not helping me keep my mind off James. Work although keeping me occupied left me with time with my thoughts, and they were running rampant.

By closing time came around I had restocked the shop, made half a dozen phone calls to clients, the warehouse, and the local newspaper to see about placing an ad in their paper for the shop. As I closed up and made sure the door was locked my mind wandered back to our last phone call. I hadn't heard from James since and I was so nervous about seeing him again. I decided to bite the bullet and phone him.

"Hi, it's me."

"Hi, princess."

"Hi princess? Hi princess? No contact for two days, and now it's *hi princess*. I'm sorry but you don't get to do that. Yes, I get it you were at the wake and were probably drunk and that's why you didn't say goodbye."

"The last time we spoke, but no communication since then"

"No text, no nothing. I'm getting pretty fed up with your yo-yo attitude towards me and your complete lack of regard for my feelings."

"Have you finished? am I allowed to speak now?"

I could hear the frustration in his voice but I didn't care.

"Is there any point in carrying on the conversation?"

"Just let me explain why I haven't been in contact."

"You've got two minutes."

"To start with it's not me that is having a complete and utter disregard for your feelings! I've just buried my father and you're going off on one at me like you've just found me in bed with another woman. Second of all, I did say goodbye, but I didn't realise my battery had died on my phone before I had said it to you, you know how dodgy the battery on it was. Remember that day you found out about Michael being in the hospital? the battery died on me then, too. Well, this week the phone finally died a death and I've had problems getting a new phone. The place I have the contract with don't have any phones in stock up where I was. I'd left my phone book at home so couldn't use someone else's phone to ring you from. I've had to wait till I got home today to sort out a new mobile. I wasn't ignoring you princess, you know you mean the world to me."

"Oh, well now I feel like a complete bitch. I'm sorry for believing the worst, and you were grieving your dad too. I understand if you can't accept my apology."

"Apology accepted, princess. Don't fret about it. listen, where are you? I'll come see you."

"I'm walking home from work."

"I'll be at yours in forty minutes, want me to bring coffee?"

"No, thank you. I'm too wired for coffee; a tea would be nice though."

"Tea and me coming right away, princess."

"I'll leave the door unlocked for you."

"Message read, loud and clear, princess."

I practically ran the rest of the way home, getting there in just under twenty minutes. My heart was racing and I was sweating in places I'd forgotten about. I spent the next fifteen minutes getting prepped and ready for him. I had the quickest shower ever and put on the fancy new underwear I had bought on my shopping trip with Corrin the other day.

I decided that the purple lace Kimono would look better just left undone, it would also provide less of an obstruction to the rest of my outfit and also to me. I had never worn anything like this before in my life, and if you'd said to me three weeks ago I'd be totally head over heels in love with a DJ and buying sexy underwear to please him, I'd have said you were bonkers.

Yet there I was, all dolled up to the nines, waiting for my DJ dreamboat to come and ravage me like some desperate housewife in a *Mills and Boon* novel. Before I knew it, I could hear his van pulling into the driveway and the door closing behind him as he came into the house.

"I'm upstairs, in the middle of something. You can come on up though."

"Ok, princess, want me to bring your tea up with me or leave it down here?"

"Leave it on the table, then come on up. I'm in the bedroom putting some clothes away."

I got on the bed as I heard him walking up the stairs and along the landing. At my bedroom though he paused before opening the door, as he stepped in his face was a picture, he was literally drooling. I shifted position on the bed as he closed the door and the gap between us. The butterflies inside me were flapping their wings causing a mini hurricane in my insides.

"Well, well, princess, if I'd known you were playing dress up for me, I'd have been here sooner."

"The tea was a rouse to give me time to get ready for you."

DJ DREAMBOAT

"Oh, I see, well they aren't going to be on you for very long."
"Shut up and kiss me."
"Yes, Ma'am."

The next two hours were the most erotic of my entire life. He took me to places I had only dreamed of. He was right though, the underwear didn't stay on me for very long, but I didn't care. His reaction as he had walked in my room had been worth every penny I'd spent on them, and now I knew what he liked I could shop online for more.

AFTERWORD

This book came about as you will be aware from the introduction as a product of a dream I had one night. There is a prominent DJ on TikTok who I watch every weekday morning. His 80's themed livestreams, play a vital part of my weekday morning routine. One morning I was listening to his livestream while catching up on the previous night's tv shows I had recorded, the music that he played on his show mixed with the show I was watching somehow seeped into my subconscious that night and subsequently DJ Dreamboat was born.

If you have ever watched the remake of Magnum P.I then you will know who I based my DJ on. If you are not I suggest a quick internet search for the actor who plays him, the gorgeous, talented Jay Hernandez. He is quite a fine looking man for certain.

Printed in Great Britain
by Amazon